SHARK

BRUCE BROOKS

A LAURA GERINGER BOOK

HarperTrophy®
A Division of HarperCollinsPublishers

Shark
Copyright © 1998 by Bruce Brooks

Library of Congress Cataloging-in-Publication Data
Brooks, Bruce.
    Shark / by Bruce Brooks.
        p.   cm. — (The Wolfbay Wings ; #6)
    "A Laura Geringer book."
    Summary: As Shark's hockey game improves and he
becomes a puck hog, he alienates himself from his teammates
and discovers that a nickname must be earned, not taken for
granted.
    ISBN 0-06-440681-4 (pbk.) — ISBN 0-06-027570-7 (lib. bdg.)
    [1. Hockey—Fiction.]   I. Title.   II. Series: Brooks, Bruce.
Wolfbay Wings ; #6.
PZ7.B7913Sh   1998   97-40270
[Fic]—dc21   CIP
                                                        AC

Typography by Steve Scott
1   2   3   4   5   6   7   8   9   10
❖
First Edition
Visit us on the World Wide Web!
http://www.harperchildrens.com

I am an ice hockey player. I go by the name of Shark.

Pretty easy to remember, isn't it? Pretty cool image to carry around. A twisting torpedo of writhing muscle. Keen with that alertness that makes intelligence seem slow. Roaming relentlessly, sharp-toothed, fight-ready, eager to slash at the slightest opening, with no conscience, no mercy, leaving no remains.

Shark. Kind of says a lot about a guy, especially when that name is chosen for him, by a bunch of tough, gritty, hardass ice hockey players who don't hand out favors to anybody.

Shark. It's a name I earned for one reason, then lost, then earned again for another. That's hard. That's work.

How did I earn it first, this name of speed and death and grace? It was easy. I earned it by being the fattest, slowest, most confused hockey player on my team, the Wolfbay Wings Squirt A's. When I tried to stickhandle, I often lost the puck and my stick as well. At least twice a game I would get spun around and my "ice sense" would tell me my team was supposed to head in the direction that was actually reserved for our opponents. I once shot on my own goalie (missed the net, but I worried him for a minute). My idea of defense was managing to drag an opponent to the ice with me as I frequently fell; my idea of playing team offense was managing to skate at least three strides (without the puck, of course) in the right direction, without going offside. I was awesome.

So the nickname was a kind of joke, as was the general name for the four or five of us who had been recruited to fill empty roster spots, and had no business on skates holding hard sticks with which we very well might injure ourselves: we were the Spazzes, or sometimes, the Spaz Line. Yes, it was a joke, but let me tell you, it was also a badge of honor. Because when I took the ice—and all of us Spazzes skated regular shifts, same as the stars—I took it without apology, without resignation, without shame. I took the ice—even in full wobble—with pride, buddy. I was a Wolfbay Wing. I wore the blue and black and white; I was one of the first three on the ice at every practice and one of the last three to leave; I worked my fins off, and if the results didn't show much at first, who cared? I was playing hockey. And one day—who could say?—one day maybe I was going to eat me some people.

But as I said, before then I had my much-treasured name cruelly taken from me by the same teammates who gave it the first time. Did that *hurt*? Oh, it hurt all right. But I had to remember the vital thing you hear about sharks: They never stop moving, never, always swimming every second, from birth to death.

Here's the story of all this tough swimmin', and how close one fat fish came to bringing it all to a very bad end and—who knows?—suffering through *next* year being called something like "Bait."

two

Because I play on a sports team now, I get to spend a lot of time with kids who, you know, just *play sports*— grew up playing sports, watched big brothers and sisters play sports, lived in houses full of sports trophies with the arms broken off, wore hand-me-down sports jerseys as plain shirts, could reach down in the middle of any floor and come up with a piece of sports equipment which they would know how to hold and handle without thinking— kids who got driven to practices and games all the time, driving that takes up twelve to twenty hours a week, by parents who just expected to do it, who shrugged and started the van and didn't imagine any other way to live—hey, the kids do *sports*, okay?

And once you notice sports, you start seeing sports *everywhere*. Open a magazine and there are pictures of ragamuffin kids in Bangladesh or Liverpool or a slum of Brisbane carrying on a soccer game with a misshapen ball made of waste from the local emergency starvation clinic, kids intent and competitive and smiling and—*goal!* Turn on your television and get sold some $200 sneakers; fold back a long, dignified page of the *Wall Street Journal* and get sold a seat at an international marketing conference with a star athlete as the keynote speaker.

It's hard for my teammates to believe what I am about to reveal, but it is the plain truth, incredible as it sounds: It is possible for a kid—even a *boy*—to get to the age of ten in this country without ever having hit a baseball with a bat or a tennis ball with a racket, caught a spiraling football or a bouncing basketball, kicked a soccer ball—and you can even grow up without *wanting* to do these things.

It doesn't happen because the kid is a scaredy nerd, a sissy, an uncoordinated doofus who can barely walk up a flight of stairs, a computer geek, or a wuss without a clue about what really matters in life. I mean, there *are* plenty of scaredy-cats and doofuses and sissies around, and they live the way they have to live, sports or no sports. But sometimes a kid who, given the chance, might really *like* sports just doesn't get a peek at that world.

In my case, as for most other sports-free kids, it was a matter of what my parents knew about and cared about. My father is a Methodist minister, a good man who reads a lot of Bible, a book in which there is very little written about soccer. My mother used to be a minor opera singer; there are very few operas about basketball. My mom developed a program for training church choirs at a very successful summer camp held just for that purpose every year. During their downtime, the kids at her camp do other things besides play catch. Anyway, *I'm* not there to play Ping-Pong; I'm working my tail off on "staff," washing dishes or assembling risers or photocopying sheet music or fitting seventy-seven music stands into a single Mitsubishi van. I'm not chillin' in front of the tube in the dorm watching the O's do something called "three-hit" the Toronto Blue Jays. . . .

I was riding in a car once with a kid whose dad, with great focus and precision, was explaining to him—at about age seven—the difference between a curveball and a slider. How the ball was held for each, how the pitcher moved his hand, wrist, elbow, shoulder, how the pitch looked coming to the plate, how it cut into the air and made its last-second deviation from the expected path. . . . It took about half an hour and the kid listened intently and asked very specific questions. The father answered carefully. It seemed pretty serious for both of them.

Well, I'm certain neither of my parents could tell me the difference between a curveball and a slider. I'd be surprised if they could tell me the difference between a baseball and a softball, even if I spotted them the color of the stitches. I can imagine them thinking, "Heavens, is *every* toss and catch and step and swing measured and analyzed like that?" And upon learning the answer was, "Oh, absolutely!" they would just think, "But—*why?*"

If you like your life, you're about as lucky as you can get. So you don't need to go further and worry about what *kind* of life you're enjoying, and what kind you are *not*. You can't really figure it out anyway; the lines that mark this life from that aren't so clear. If I were a little less alert, I could be excused for being *shocked* at how many families out there don't know a perfect fifth held three measures with vibrato from a diminished fifth faded over three measures without vibrato. It just depends on who you get for parents.

My mother made sure I had the chance to listen to a lot of music as a kid, and I really took to it for reasons I actually do not remember anymore. Somehow I decided at an alarmingly early age that I wanted to play the oboe. So the oboe became my "extra thing" aside from schoolwork (I go to a church school) and church activities and friendships. I took oboe lessons, played recitals, went to music camps, entered music competitions, traveled with an orchestra, went through six different teachers, got to beat the absolute living crud, oboe to oboe, out of a snakehearted rival who had been mean and cocky to me for three years—listen, I had a ball. I just never *threw* one.

Then last spring I applied to a very prestigious summer study program. The application process involved three recitals, one of them in front of a world-famous conductor named Daniel Barenboim, which I aced, and two interviews.

As the date for acceptances neared, my parents grew nervous. Then my mother received a very unusual phone call. The director of the program happened to be in town seeing to some business about grants, and he wondered if she could spare him half an hour in his hotel's coffee shop. Astonished, she agreed to go.

The headmaster, she later reported, was very gracious, and bought her a pot of tea, after inquiring if she preferred herbal; he also offered her a pastry, which she declined. Then he had a nice, long, frank talk with her about me. Basically, he explained that my musicianship and what he called my "general character" made me a "very fine" candidate for the program. But, he regretted to say, the decision of the admissions committee had been to defer acceptance for a year, possibly two.

Why? asked my mom, completely perplexed.

Because, the headmaster explained, no doubt very delicately, he and the head of the winds faculty really thought I would benefit from a life in which I did something besides play the skinny horn and go to church.

My mother says she then knew two things at once: first, that I would never be a particularly special musician, because these people want *those* kids to give up everything *but* their instrument; and, second, she knew the director was right about my life, and that she and my dad would have no idea what to do about it.

I won't go through all of the comical attempts my parents made in a spirit of total willingness and beneficence to allow me to choose some new activity that would broaden my experience of the well-rounded oboist's life. You'll get an idea of how far they were prepared to go when I tell you that my father, the Methodist minister whose idea of a hot night is an impassioned discussion of Solomon with two of his younger "radical" deacons, took me to a full-blown superstar-lineup big-wheel-truck demolition derby in an arena filled with shrieking rednecks. *And* bought me a red cap with yellow letters on it that said MY WHEELS ARE BIGGER THAN YOUR HOUSE. I never had the heart to wear it.

One day one of the mothers who drives my music-lesson carpool got messed up in her scheduling and had to stop on the way home to pick up her younger son, who was just finishing his ice hockey practice at a nearby rink. Probably because I didn't want to spend any time alone with her daughter, a snooty violinist, I decided to dash in with the mother as she picked up her kid.

It was like seeing the ocean for the first time. Or mountains. Or your very first comic book.

I'm sure my mouth dropped open and did not shut until I was somehow guided back to the car.

I arrived home and announced to my parents that my horizons were at last about to broaden. When I told them what I wanted to do, I think my father, at least, was relieved. My mother was puzzled. But the fact that I would at least have to learn to ice-skate gave her something to be pleased about. So I had their full support. They started The Project of finding me a team right away. And, as I have already explained, I was lucky enough to end up a Wing.

Now, if only I could remember why I used to like that oboe so much. . . .

three

One thing I can tell you about kids who have not played sports: they have absolutely no idea how many muscles they possess, or how many joints, and they have no idea that these things—and probably lots of sinews and tendons and cartilage too, whatever there is—can be moved to *extremes*.

It takes only one practice to get an idea. One practice plus one night's sleep. The next morning is when you start to take note of these new body parts that you use to, well, *play*. . . .

This is not to say that people who don't wear uniforms with numbers on the backs several times a year are slack, poorly toned sacks of barely used protoplasm. Plenty of non-athletes seem to be in fine shape, hale and rosy-cheeked and strong of breath and sinew. I suppose I am saying that athletics finds the extremes, and makes them become more the norm for a body part's function. Obviously this can be bad—that's why we see these ex-pro athletes every now and then in a magazine or on a TV show, decayed and arthritic and looking 53 at 35. But Squirt hockey players are not called on to make quite the dire sacrifices professionals are. So I'm not at all ready to say it's not good for me to find out that I am in fact a great deal more flexible than I thought in the shoulder and hip, capable of far greater leverage through the knee and elbow and wrist, holding, as if in conscious restraint, far greater muscular power in the thigh, the arm, the hand. So far, I have faith it will all add up to *additions*, not subtractions.

But oh, for a while at least, it *does* hurt. It hurts with an interior surprise that makes you question whether or not you really have been living *in* your own body or perhaps, have just been kind of using it from the outside like a marionette or something, to enact what you were doing more than to feel it.

When your thigh muscles feel electrified from skating lines, when your ankles ache from trying to stay upright without a wobble, when a slapshot from behind you hits the back of your knee and raises a welt like a Very-Hard pink rubber eraser—you *feel* it all. You can do nothing else sometimes.

four

"Shoot it shoot it shoot it," bellows Coach Cooper, as close as he gets to screaming. But I hold the puck on my stick too long, looking for *something*—someone better to pass it to, perhaps—and the defenseman, Barry, who placed himself badly out of position by falling for a fake shot by Prince and diving to the ice to block it because Zip, the goalie, was himself lying down, having stopped a slapshot from Woodsie that rebounded to Prince . . . well, they get it to me, and I hold the puck instead of shooting it, Barry clambers back up and stumble-skates back over to where I stand politely waiting to hand the thing over to him, and he chops it off my stick and starts skating away with it, and like it's an afterthought puts his right glove in my face mask and shoves, and I fall down.

Coach blows his whistle. I climb up. He is massaging the bridge of his nose, looking wearied.

"Nice recovery, Barry," he says, without stopping the massage. "And nice fake, Prince."

Prince isn't quite satisfied with this compliment. "Put the man *flat*," he elaborates. "Got his concave chest *cold*."

"I'd've swatted your wimpy shot like a ladybug if you hadn't had the sense to give it up," says Barry.

I suspect they are both covering for me with their banter. The coach's weariness is one I have often seen. I have usually caused it, by failing to shoot the puck when, through some unlikely sequence of flukes, I end up with it on my stick, inches from the cage, often with the goalie out of position. The coach lets Prince and Barry trade insults until they run out of things to say, and then there is nothing to do but look up at me—in fact, by this time, everyone on the ice is looking at me—and say, "Shark. Shoot the puck."

"Sure, Coach," I say brightly, as if this were the first time he had made such a suggestion, and the first time I had considered it.

"Most players . . ." He shakes his head, then looks around until he locates Boot. "Boot. Can you, as a favor to me, try to imagine a situation in which you would *not* try to put the puck in the goal?"

Boot—overcoming his disgust at my lack of drive to score in situations he *prays* for—stands and thinks. A couple of times he seems to have come up with an answer, a situation in which he wouldn't shoot, and he raises a hand and starts to speak. But then he evidently solves the problem and imagines a possible method of shooting, and shakes his head.

The coach says, "Boot, if you were on your knees at the red line, facing away from the goal we shoot at, and one guy was lying across your legs and another guy had your left arm twisted behind you, and your stick had just broken and you had only about eighteen inches of straight wood in your right hand, and the puck suddenly appeared, whizzing past you at a bad angle and wobbling too, would you get off a shot?"

"Of course," Boot says. "That's easy. First, I'd use my elbow to—"

"Thanks. I'm sure you've got it all worked out, and I'm sure you'd probably at least cause a rebound." He looks at me. "The point is—Jeez, this year I have even gotten *Prince* to shoot more.

"Prince," Coach Cooper says to him, "how many goals you got?"

"I have no idea," says Prince, subtly but definitely conveying how very distasteful he feels it would be for him to know.

"No, sorry, of course you don't. Boot—how many goals does Prince have?"

"He has twenty-seven goals in league play," says Boot without hesitation.

"Thank you," says Coach Cooper, looking back at me. "Now. Shark. Let me ask you. *How*? *How* did Prince—who as we all know would rather make a pretty pass than eat ice cream—*how* do you think Prince got all those goals?"

"That's easy," I say, straightfaced. "He stole them all from Boot."

Everyone on the ice, except Boot, who even manages a wounded smile, cracks up, and the practice drifts off without the lecture ever being finished. But Coach knows he made his point. And he knows Barry made it even better than he did.

As I get dressed, I imagine Coach Cooper is probably somewhere in the building wondering whether he should have nailed his point about my need to shoot. But I'll bet he knows that finishing the talk is not necessary—finishing the shot *is*. My problem is a little peculiar and a little complicated, but I believe we both understand it very well.

It has nothing to do with "fear." I am not afraid of being stopped by the goalie, I am not afraid of missing the net. I am not afraid of "failing"—for one thing, I have pulled off highwire auditions where the pressure was far greater, because my proficiency was so much greater; and for another, I *do* in fact "fail," by *not* shooting.

It is more a problem of stopping to think. Here is what happens. Thanks to Coach Cooper's philosophy of regularly mixing the makeup of lines so that periodically a Spaz will get to play alongside much better players, and partly thanks to . . . well, frankly, I don't really know, I sometimes—even often—seem to have made a couple of moves, knocked a couple of bodies, spun this way or that, looked in the right direction, and somehow managed to wind up somewhere around the doorstep of the goal, alone with the puck and a clear shot. It is then that I freeze.

On occasion, I have pulled the trigger. The

results: a modest five goals, which total leads the Spaz Line by a huge margin. I *like* scoring. I *like* being pounded, having my name hollered by lots of guys, having my fellow Spazzes muster all of their coordination in order to whack the boards from their seats on the bench without sailing their sticks out onto the ice. It's great. Let's do it some more. No problem.

But—well, there *does* seem to be a problem, doesn't there?

Part of it may be that Spazzes shouldn't get too ambitious. It was not lost upon me that by being a member of the Wings who could not really play hockey, I was enjoying the pleasure of belonging to *two* groups: the Wings, and the Spazzes.

It might be interesting to do a study of great teams of the past to see how they treated the worst players on their team. Did the coaches and players just kind of dismiss them with indifference, giving them very little ice time in games, putting up with them at practices, generally ignoring them? What, say, if the worst kid on the team was also the funniest in terms of locker-room humor—would he be enjoyed for his jokes if he didn't earn the right to be funny first on the ice? I'm sure at least some of the kids scorned the worst players and mocked them openly—in fact, I've seen it happen.

Personally, if such a study were made, I hope it shows that great teams treat their worst players with respect and all that sort of thing. I would not expect any other team to treat its bad players the way the Wings treat us, with respect, amusement, and a complete lack of impatience. We get to play regular shifts, which I have overheard more than one parent complaining about to Coach Cooper, especially if a Spaz Line was on the ice at the end of a close game or something. This means the other players know they simply *have* to put up with us. And although we do our share to contribute, the losses are not due to Spaz misplays entirely. Everybody helps, except maybe four or five guys who make very few mistakes.

I noticed that some of the Spazzes seemed to be making no real attempt to get better at hockey. Coach Cooper took part of every practice to go over ridiculously fundamental things with us, especially when we messed up during drills that basically served everyone else as warm-ups. Some guys listened, tried again, failed again, laughed, and let it go. In games they kind of stood around generally in position, and tried to skate to their next position when the puck changed zones, but if they fell they got up slow and laughing, and didn't particularly bust their butts making up for the lost time. They were Spazzes—what could anybody expect?

I didn't quite feel this way. Never did I tell anyone—certainly not my fellow incompetents—that I couldn't just stay in one place as a kind of clown, but felt instead that I had to make *some* effort to learn and get better. I could only do so much though—I was a Spaz to the bones, and even if I picked up a new insight or half a skill, I was in no danger of being elevated to "full player" status. This was good. I confess I was very relieved to have nobody expecting anything of me. I was kind of secretive about what I picked up—mostly because it wasn't much and I didn't put it into play with sudden adroitness. But also because I didn't want anybody counting on my being able to do something I could not, at a crucial time. I wasn't hiding behind my incompetence, I don't think, but I definitely hung on to it as a kind of protection against responsibility.

Some players *did* notice, nonetheless. Once Dooby came up to me as we skated to the gate at the end of practice, clapped me on the shoulder, and said, "Way to go, Sharkster!"

I looked at him in genuine perplexity. "What do you mean?"

"You never fell tonight," he said. "Not once. Not during drills or the whole scrimmage. Keep that skating going!" Then he slid ahead of me through the gate. I was pleased and horrified at the same time. Pleased, because I had evidently stayed upright. Horrified, because somebody was watching, somebody noticed.

Later, after a scrimmage, after I had missed three straight leading passes from Prince, he scooted next to me on the bench and said, "Hey, I'm not talkin' because it was me gave you those passes and I'm mad you didn't convert them into assists, okay? This has nothing to do with me; it's about receiving passes, okay?" I said okay, and he proceeded to give me a very simple tip about making sure that when I crossed the blue line for an onside pass I had adjusted my stride so that my body was "open" (chest to the inside), which meant my stick arm was forward and had better reach, rather than "closed" (back to the inside), which meant my stick arm was back and my reach was way reduced.

I was glad for the tip, grateful for the attention, and Prince graciously refused my every effort to apologize for flubbing his setups. At the same time I was now extremely worried that I was expected to make it to every lead pass and take it cleanly on my forehand.

For a while, it was still the case, and very comfortably so, that if during a scrimmage or especially a game I made a decently important play with decent success, the thing was treated as a gift from heaven, a blissful accident greeted with howls of laughter, feigned incredulity, and a general sense that at least once in a while a snakebit team found a piece of luck.

Cody, holding his huge bag over his shoulder and changing the cassette in his tape player at the same time with the hand holding his sticks, manages to swat my leg as he passes. Without looking, he says what he always says: "Play a little hockey, Sharko."

Play hockey. Not "Shoot the puck, Sharko." Of

course, to say such a thing to me could be equated with my slapping a clueless third-grade band student on the back and saying, "Play a little music, kid." But I think Cody means something. However, it doesn't pay to think too hard about things Cody says. Leaving a practice one weeknight, he passed Ernie, a near-Spaz in his second year who is called "Dead" because Cody once heard someone use the phrase "in dead earnest," and Codes said, "Remember, Dead: Sleep naked."

And he was gone. Personally, I bet Ernie slept naked that night. Perhaps he still does, and will continue to do so, until Cody nudges him in a scrimmage one day and says, "Oh, and, Dead—get back with the jammies thing, 'kay? Naked is, like, over."

n my father, I have always admired an ability he possesses, to do things without ever really taking responsibility for them first, when taking that responsibility would have seemed *personal*, perhaps aggressive or presumptuous or showy. The responsibility was like an extra step that could be simply skipped, in perfect humility; nothing need be said, no one's dependence need be brought out; no promise need be made against which others would be required to judge any good that might otherwise be simply accepted. This is a kind of grace that I suppose marks the best clergymen who, in all sincerity, see themselves as accomplishing nothing, but merely being blessedly available for this or that task God first conceives, then embodies in the world, then solves through some use of a man's intelligence or strength or subtlety or insight, all of which are merely reflections of His own unfathomably greater qualities.

When a Spaz is not quite a Spaz anymore, is it possible that he can simply be a humble tool or vehicle like this, allowing the greater qualities of the team to flow through him when he happens to be fortunate enough to get in its path? If so, does the player need to take credit, encourage dependence, offer promise? Or can he merely let himself be animated, as his ability allows, by the will and ambition and skill and far smarter designs of his teammates and coach?

It is not necessarily fear that makes a fellow decline the chance to assume what looks like personal responsibility. It can be humility.

And it is not fear that makes a fellow humble.

six

A rare day. It finally happened. First, one of my parents— my father, as it happens—has driven me to our home game against York this Saturday morning. Usually I ride with another player or Coach Cooper picks me up. Second, instead of dropping me off, my father has stayed, sitting in one place the whole time (though he has brought several manuscripts, probably of sermons, and of course a Bible, to riffle through and read while the game clock is ticking). And last, I make a play. I make, in fact, a drop-dead grandstand play and score the game-winning goal with one minute remaining and stun everyone in the building, none more than the two poor saps I victimize on the opposition.

It happens this way. After about ninety seconds on the ice, Java is carrying the puck at midspeed across the red line with his linemates nearby, and Coach Cooper makes the obvious move and hollers

"Change!" Java slaps the puck down the boards as he skates to the bench, and it ends up behind the cage, where the York defenseman knows that, because of our line change, he has plenty of time to fetch it, and pass it out to his unchecked wing on the half-boards. The wing will then carry it over the blue line into the neutral zone, where in all likelihood our new line is just getting onto the ice and someone will have sense enough to give him a token diversion—a poke, a hook, a swat, anything to hold him up for a second—while we get organized for his team's passage into our zone.

This play happens, just as I have told it, probably fifty times a game. It is so routine it's dull, especially by the end of a game. And if, like today, the game is tied—a decent result for both teams, no need to press anything.

Aha—but not if your team happens to feature the rapacious, ever-hungry, thousand-toothed Shark, and he happens to have stepped onto the wood strip that is the jamb of the on-ice door instead of waiting on the bench side of it (requiring that he lift his skates over it one after the other and place them flat onto the ice), and thus when his turn comes he is actually standing *above* the ice surface and can push off the jamb directly onto the ice with something called *momentum*, and furthermore finds that in trying to avoid two of his own guys coming to the bench he has set this momentum going right along the boards, which, when he looks up, he sees is bringing him up rather fast to the York wing about to receive his lazy pass from behind the net, the wing with his head looking back and down for the puck, because no one *ever* gets in there and checks him—

Prince and Woodsie later describe the play for me a hundred times, and they insist I did it all as one smooth piece of pure hockey, but I don't remember it that way. Apparently, just as the winger turned his head, with his stick held out on the ice-side with the puck open on the blade, natural as could be, I loomed into his vision like a sudden ghost and his eyes got huge. Prince swears I said "Boo!" but I will never believe it. In any case, just as I planted my right shoulder in the winger's unsuspecting chest I chopped downward with my stick and popped the puck perfectly up off his blade and on the way, roughly with me, toward the York goal.

The next part gets tough to pin down, because for me it was the part that happened fastest as well as being the part that seems least possible, whereas for my observers it was the most distinctive and therefore best-registered part of all. Anyway: There I was, skating by now at my full speed toward the suddenly ready goalie who had gotten his wits together enough to come out and challenge me, and, my trouble is, I am a little ahead of the puck, which is still kind of floating on a bounce. But instead of doing what any *common* hockey player would do in this spot—which is, of course, try to control the puck with the blade of one's stick, at the expense of having the stick settled in readiness for a shot—I, the Shark, nothing in my body but muscle and cartilage, keep *my* stick on the ice, settled and ready to shoot, and, unbelievable as it sounds (but I have never known Woodsie to lie), I calmly lift my back skate and kick the puck out of the air ahead of me and onto my stick blade, which I then use as it should be used, to flick the biscuit between the goalie's pads for the gamewinner. As Zip says, "No perspiration." I mean, what could be more natural, really?

* * *

The poor York players are still scratching their helmets as the buzzer sounds and I begin my brief reign as king of the freaking rink. I am lost in a flurry of howls and poundings and punches to the head, my stick is snatched (by Cody, who informs me that I have just established, by becoming its only member, the Spaz Hall of Fame, of which The Stick is the sole exhibit), I am even given an extra pat by the no doubt furious York coach (York has beaten us three times this year; I recall only the first score, which was 17–2) and am told, by him, that I possess "smart feet." I am borne off the ice in a mass of yowling, sweaty, triumphant boys who don't let my skates touch the ice all the way to the gate, or the floor all the way to the locker room. In vain I try to signal my father that I will be out in a little while, but my arms are pinned and I just see his perplexed face, looking up from papers he has been drawn away from for probably too long an interval, and then I am past. I know he did not see the shot, nor, probably, was he aware of what happened, though I'm sure he did check the scoreboard and saw that we won. It's really okay if he missed the big play. Even if he had been watching, with complete concentration, I don't think he would have understood. Hey, I *did* it, and I don't understand. Still—he *was* right here and all. If only he had looked up. . . .

Dooby, in only his cupholder, stands on a bench and announces that I have now scored more goals than Barry has amassed in his entire career, to which Barry snorts, "He's welcome to 'em," while adding quietly to me, "Nice play." Boot, who I can never figure, does a very quick and funny number on me to assess my threat to his own goal-greed. And of course everyone beats Coach Cooper to it by hollering in unison as he enters, "Shark! Shoot the puck, Shark!" The ref sticks his head in the door and hands something to the coach with a quick couple of words, and a minute later the coach slips me a puck. *The* puck, apparently. For a moment I am humiliated that the referee could recognize it was so unusual for me to make a decent play that he would go to the trouble of retrieving a souvenir for me. But I look up and see Dooby shaking his head.

"I know what you're thinking," he says. "But,

see, it's not cuz you're a Spaz. *That* was a play to remember for *anyone*, you dork."

"But . . . but I just—" I stammer.

"Just let us treat you for a few minutes as if you were a hockey player, and then we can all get back to normal," says Zip. He looks down to fuss with a buckle, but I know goalies, and I know Zip, so I know he can't help adding, "He should have closed the fiver on you. Even though, you know, it *was* a nice play and all."

Just as Barry is saying, "Zip pees in his pads every time the puck crosses the blue line and says, 'It's not *supposed* to do that,'" my father sticks his head in the door. He catches my eye and tries to smile and say that he heard something about how I—when the guys nearest the door pull him in and six of them start talking to him at once, all as if they had known him as an uncle since birth, all of them undressing without a thought, and cussing carelessly, and then even more join in, all ritually mocking my play, and my poor dad just stands there with one hand in a pocket and the other clutching papers, blushing and nodding, and having a hard time trying to squeeze in a *smile*, much less a word. Coach Cooper figures out who he is and grabs his hand, but he has already let the hand go by the time my dad alerts himself to the fact that he is Meeting My Coach and that therefore it is important he do it well. By then Coach Cooper is hollering something cruel to Shinny about his broken wrist, and my father slips even further out to sea. I quickly knot my second shoe, hoist my bag, yell, "Eat your hearts out, you bunch of bottom feeding *fish*," and then I go and rescue my dad by taking his arm and gently pulling him with me out of the room. The door closes on a whole new series of jeers in response to mine.

"Hi, Pop," I say. "Ready to go?"

He studies me quickly, nodding. "Do I understand that congratulations . . . I'm sorry not to . . . it's possible I was . . ."

"No sweat." I tell myself it really isn't. I put my hand up on his shoulder and we walk down the hall to the door. Four or five players or coaches from other Wings teams who were watching our game nod and smile or even say, "Nice play." My father leaves off his attempt to explain, or perhaps to understand, and it's all okay. I am incredibly happy.

"Please," he says as he opens the door for me to clatter through with sodden bag snocking me on one side and uneven stick blades spearing the other, "please tell me—*what* is it they call you?"

"Shark," I say. He frowns. His reaction reminds me that I have never told my mother the name either. "Don't worry; it's a very honorable nickname." He still looks doubtful. "Hey," I say, "do you remember that red-headed minister who came to a couple of revivals? I recall him saying something cool once, something about 'the mockery that loves.'"

"But they mock you by calling you Shark because—?"

"Because generally, Dad, I'm what you might call a complete flounder."

"Ah." He nods and gives my arm a consoling squeeze. Then he frowns a little. "But surely they realize this is your first—"

"They do," I say. "They expect nothing. That's why the mockery is an honor."

"Of course. Of course. That—well, all is good, then. You—" He searches for words as we walk. "They really do *like* you. Not that I'm surprised, no one knows more than I how—"

"They do," I say, "and you're right, the jive is for all the right reasons."

"Then I don't know whether I am prouder of *you*," he says with the hint of a smile, extracting his keys, "or of *them*, for being perceptive."

"I think I can safely say 'Thank you' on their behalf as well as mine."

When we finally stop next to the car—and even then, while he searches for the right key, we are subjected to a hail of abuse from five or six Mite A players who razz me across the parking lot—he settles in, gives a sigh, and asks simply, "Sebastian, my dear boy, as to the game itself: Tell me the truth. What is that special thing that happened?"

"Well," I start. He watches me, waiting. No, I cannot do it. "Well, we won." I say. "Which we do very seldom, see."

"Ah. Yes." His eyes close with relief. He is thinking that he *did* understand after all. He doesn't usually speak while driving, but today he chatters, politely telling me how much he enjoyed "being present"—bless him, my father would never lie by saying he enjoyed "watching" when he knows very well he did no such thing—and getting to see some of my "new milieu."

"Sorry about the profanity," I say.

He pretends not to have any idea what I mean, choosing instead to say, "*And* I had the chance to meet your coach, who seems to be a very nice man, with excellent leadership qualities. . . ."

I love this guy. What do I care how a slider works?

A little while later, during a silence at a red light, I ask, "What's the sermon tomorrow?" His eyes brighten. *Now* we're talkin'. It seems, he says, that he had the most *revealing* intuition about how two separate texts might be read in opposition— well, not a personal *intuition*, of course; a little grace freely sent from the source of all inspiration, of course. . . .

When we get home I hand my mom the puck without a word and head for the kitchen. She catches up with me as I root in the refrigerator, rolling the strange hard disc around her hand, frowning at it, sniffing it once (which I love to see her do; pucks smell *good*, essence of vulcanized rubber), glancing up at me several times.

"Every single one is made in one place in the Czech Republic," I tell her, before swigging some apple juice straight from the quart bottle. "Every single one. For, like, seventy-five years, no changes in the thing. How would you like to be, say, the director of design there, at the puck factory, the puckworks? In the puck *town*? Generations pass. 'It was good enough for your great grandfather . . .'" I burp too slightly to excuse myself.

"Thank you," she says, holding it up.

"Sure, Mom," I say, and those are the only words we ever speak about my hero day.

an a person be proud of something he does in the course of a sporting contest—a very good play made at the right time, relative to the other players' positions and the game's special "time," which has nothing to do with real time—and still claim to hold on to his larger sense of the world and its problems—and his own lack of achievement in solving any of them? Is a game just a kind of artificial world unto itself, inside which one can do good things or bad things, with the comfort of complete meaninglessness? But what about the emotions one inspires in one's teammates and opponents—don't these feelings (loyalty, pride in others, faith, dependence, fondness, or the base opposites of these good emotions, as held against kids who simply happen to be wearing shirts of a different color) really occur and last and matter?

Or are the feelings one inspires purely by sports actions insignificant and quick to vanish in the light of day, nothing but imitations of the real thing? Does the nameless feeling—almost a kind of love—that tickles my chest whenever I see Prince carrying the puck as he skates in a low-angled circle through our zone with his eyes seeming more than alive with intelligence and desire . . . does this feeling, which I feel at least three or four times a game, always as if for the first time, or the chill of amazed pride I feel when my fellow rookie Woodsie invents a pass of genius, and delivers it in the form of a puck that somehow arrives at the stick of the receiver with a softness of touch, a rightness of spin, a kindness of angle—are these all just transitory admirations? Do I need to see Prince working in a soup kitchen for the homeless one Saturday, or Woodsie wheeling MS patients around the city park in their wheelchairs?

las for my glory—soon enough I had to find it was pretty inflated. It was Zip who gave me the first hints; it was Zip who delivered the first full message, near the end of a scrimmage a week or so later. I had whacked in a one-timer early on, as the trailer of a two-on-two, Cody and Boot against Dooby and Ernie. Now, with maybe three minutes left before Zamboni time, I slid to the edge of the crease unnoticed by Woodsie, who was playing too far toward the corner because he thought the puck was going to pop out that way any second. So there I am, smiling benevolently on the guys hacking away in the corner, confident that my center would come up with the puck and center it right over here to little ol' scorin' machine Me and *wham*.

I hit the ice flat on my back. The puck *did* come shooting through, but Zip took it on his forehand and wristed it to center ice.

I lay there. He looked down at me.

"What's your problem?" he said. "Get the freak up. In case you didn't know, there's a guy on the other side you're supposed to be checking and"—he looked up and squinted—"right now he's jumping into a three-on-two."

"Was that *you?*" I said.

"Was that I who took exception to you putting your butterball in my face and standing all happy and relaxed in my crease? Yes, as a matter of fact, it *was* I. Who tripped *you.*"

I climbed up. They had scored at the other end, so there was a break. The back of my head hurt; I tried to ignore it and laugh, but the laugh sounded pretty thin. "But why bother tripping *me?*"

He stared at me hard on that one. Then he finally said, "Why shouldn't I bother? Tell me."

I laughed. It didn't feel any better standing up. "Since when do you allow yourself to be so concerned with Spazzes?"

He shook his head and said, "Tsk-tsk," dramatically, as he swept ice to his posts, stick swinging side to side. He stopped, hit the angle of the stick into the pocket of his catching glove, looked at me, shook his head again. "Such a shame," he said.

"What's up, Zip?"

He sighed again. "To see a young player with promise—not much, it's true, not much at all—but still . . . of course, *sometimes* derogatory names are used to hide behind—"

I laughed. "But *I* didn't make it up. *You've* called *me* a Spaz all year and you know it."

He swept some more ice. "Anybody called you that lately?" he asked. He looked up and made a dismissive gesture with his stick. "Stop calling *yourself* old names as an excuse to loaf, or they won't be calling you 'Shark' for long either. Now get out of here."

Loaf? Me? I laughed to myself—I wasn't *good* enough to loaf! Was I? These goals and things just kind of dropped onto the ice in front of me; I had no idea how to *earn* them.

During the remainder of that scrimmage, three things happened that were new. First, Cody yelled at me—really yelled at me—for not messing with the stick of the man I was checking, letting him receive a pass and fire a hard shot (which the goalie saved). I was speechless—at his anger, and at his presumption that I would even *think* to mess with a guy's stick to ruin his shot.

Second and third, I got hit, hard, on two occasions when I was carrying the puck in the neutral zone and looked down to get it out of my skates. The second hit was from Woodsie, and it made my molars ache.

Looking down, Woodsie seemed indecisive for a second. "Sorry," he said, and started to skate away. Then he swerved back, and in the same polite voice said, "Actually, I take that back, Shark. I'm actually *not* sorry."

"It was a pretty nasty hit to lay on a Spaz," I said.

"Hmm," said Woodsie, and skated away.

I thought about it. It's true that lately I had been skating pretty much every shift with good players, most of them with Shinny at center. And he was getting me the puck, and I was scoring, more and more. But it was so easy, as I said. In the first period of the first game of the season's final month, Shinny had threaded a very pretty pass through two defensemen to me and I poked it in. In the third period he did exactly the same thing and I had exactly the same chance, but I flubbed it off the side of the net. As he and I skated up ice, I chuckled and made some self-mocking Spaz comment like, "At least I dribbled it in the right direction."

But Shinny snarled, "What are you *laughing* at, brick-stick? You'll never *get* a sweeter setup. Certainly not from *me* again."

"Hey, come on," I said. "Take it easy, Shins. I put the first one home, didn't I?"

"And what was so different about the second one?" he said, and darted off to poke-check a rushing defenseman.

In one game I had six shots on goal. Go figure. In the third game I *scored* twice. Both were easy shots from in close, put in after someone else had done most of the work, so I didn't exactly feel like the Skating Ace out there. After the second of the goals in that game, I passed Boot on the bench. He sat, as always when waiting his turn, straight and unsmiling, alert only to the game. I always liked that about him. He concentrated off the ice as much as he did on it.

"Better watch it, Bootster," I panted, dropping onto the bench.

He flicked a glance at me, then went back to watching the game. "What does that mean?" he asked.

"I'm closing in," I said. "Picking them off, one by one. Every goal I get is one you don't, right? I mean, isn't that what you said once, when Cody scored four in a game and Dooby asked why you were frowning?"

Boot flicked me another quick look and made a profane and unmistakably hostile suggestion. I felt my chest go hollow.

"Hey," I managed to say. "Hey, Boot. Come on. I was only joking. You know that."

"Goals and jokes don't go together," he said. Then he gave me a longer look that seemed to say, "Make your choice, if you haven't already."

But it took Prince getting mad at me during a scrimmage to finally send the message home. Standing in the low slot, I missed two centering passes on one shift because on the first, Woodsie neatly lifted my stick, and on the second, he just as neatly pinned it flat to the ice.

Prince skated right up to me. "Let me ask you something," he panted, and I could hear a beautiful but scary tremble of fury just below the surface of his voice.

"Sure," I said. "Nice pass, by the way. Sorry—"

"Have you ever taken Woodsie or Dooby or Barry aside for three or four minutes here and there at practices and said, 'Okay, let's play with the sticks,' and gone at it, fought it out *hard*, as if it were real, even for a short time? And at the end maybe you even asked them how you could beat one of their tricks that gave you trouble?"

"Well . . . no," I said, starting to smile as if the very idea were ridiculous. "I mean, I can *really* see Dooby taking me seriously if I wobbled over to him and asked for some help on the finer points—"

"Oh, don't give me this 'wobble' crap," he snapped. "I don't want excuses. How come *you* do?" He glared at me and skated away.

Behind me I heard Woodsie's soft voice, speaking low in such a way that I knew better than to turn around. Woodsie doesn't intrude much, he's even apologetic telling you your skate lace is untied, so I just listened. He said, "I don't think . . . I mean, if I were you, Shark, I'd notice that, really, you know, there's nobody on this team that can't be taken seriously. And, again if I were you, I'd think hard about how that applies to you. You know? Um, sorry if it's not my business . . ." He quietly whisked away.

nine

One Saturday morning I wake up and realize this hockey season is almost over. I get out of bed and squint at the schedule taped to the wall above my desk. Yep. Not quite three weeks left of practice and games. Three weeks! I remember when—for various reasons—it seemed the season would last for years.

One reason is that I was so new and uncertain of even being able to take the ice, there was nothing assured about each upcoming game, no chance to feel routine about the rolling progress of a six-month season. Every game was like its own adventure, its own season, starting in suspense, ending in relief.

I used to groan. When the first one escaped me I was shocked; I had always thought groans were found only in novels. But no. Before starting my hockey work each week, I groaned, deep and long, from the heart. From the ankles, shoulders, heels, and butt, too.

Of course, this began to change, as I got more sure of myself—of at least being able to play at the level of minimal requirement, and mostly as the team started coming together. The team *did* come together and that saved us from unimaginable private miseries. I had played my oboe in chamber groups and orchestras, and certainly there is a feeling of collective work, mutual support, shared respect in music. I had even played one free-improv concert with the Wings. But my musical groups were *nothing* like this brotherhood, where very little was said but within which you could find yourself, in a comfortable and complex crossfire of feelings and "surface words" covering everything—expectation, patience, affection that was far from automatic, loyalty, faith, respect for privacy, support in the group, critique, praise (not always oblique, either), dependence, and, literally above all, *attention*—you knew you could slip *nothing* by these guys, no sulk ("Hey, looks like tonight's the night Barry does the overdose with the sleeping pills." "Got enough, Bare?"), no funk, no blissy mood ("Hey, guys, Woodsie's smiling again, I think it's happy-just-to-be-here time." "Somebody go put Tiger Balm in his cup"), no self-pity or self-congratulation, no secrets (even private remorses that were left private—death in the family, an alcoholic parent's weekend in jail, a brother busted for drugs—were at least known, acknowledged, so their privacy could be clearly vouchsafed). For me, what was so wonderful was that I never had to sit outside this group and figure out how to get in and fit; all I had to do was show up and not try to be someone I wasn't—very similar to not trying to make a play you cannot on the ice— and the work was done for me, around me. I had to pass a few tests, most of them related to humor, and the degree of abuse you could bear before you made the mistake of taking some cruel joke seriously and getting angry or—far worse—hurt. That was one thing everybody made clear: There might be times when they would be willing to make you angry. But there would probably never be a time when they would be willing to make you just hurt. At least I could not imagine it.

If it had been left to me, I would never have been able to figure out a place for myself on this team. I would never have known what to show, when to joke, when to voice rank homilies with sincerity, when to linger, when to hurry. . . . But it was all taken care of, and somehow I was clearly and carefully made aware, as if by codes drummed at night in the forest rather than by words, of just who I was and what I did and what was needed from me.

Early on, the season had seemed as if it were going to be like a long prison sentence: every game was a humiliating defeat. Especially bad was the fact that we were not even getting to handle the puck enough to *play*. Even to Cody and Dooby and Prince, our best players, it felt as if the Wings were at the rink just to stand like cardboard cutouts on the ice, and let the other team's hotshots practice maneuvers around us. It was horrible. How we got through that time I am not sure I know, and I am not sure I even want to remember it enough to do the thinking. We sucked. We were ashamed. But we did keep showing up at the rink . . .

Then, the team started coming together and we started playing better hockey, started competing for some games. Our team feeling began to show up in passes, hits, coverage for missed checks, pucks won in the corners, goals scored on third rebounds. We refused to take the punishment or the disrespect. No slight was allowed to pass without a price exacted. No move against us came easy. We were arrogant whenever possible. We taunted and sneered and intimidated along with the best of them. After a short while, we started to hate losing. We started to hate tying. We started to expect to win.

And we started to win.

And—here I smile—I started to score goals.

I look at my schedule, yawning. Of our previous six games we have won four. That's incredible, or would have been incredible five months before. As it is, I resent the two losses, one of which could have been a tie if I had simply swept in a rebound that landed at my feet in the third period, one of which would have been a victory if Zip hadn't let in two long shots, but as far as I was concerned every goalie, especially Zip, was allowed to have bad days whenever they came.

The stars of the team—Cody, Prince, Boot, Barry, Dooby, Zip, maybe Woodsie even though he was a rookie, maybe Shinny even though he had missed quite a few games—had just kept playing splendidly, and let the rest of us slowly try to catch up. I saw those players as having played an incredibly consistent season all the way through the center of an overall experience of near chaos, not just for me but for everyone, including Coach Cooper. Those players, the leaders, have managed to be tough on the rest of us without asking *too* much, and without ever establishing a cruel hierarchy— we're the stars, you're the hacks—that would have let them off the hook for the year. But the stars also didn't pretend they were *not* better than most of us. The we're-all-doing-our-best-and-I-just-got-lucky stuff would have been the worst kind of condescension, and I doubt even the Spazzes would have stood for it. And the Spazzes will stand for almost anything.

For a second I am nagged by a memory—more an intuition, really—of something unpleasant, triggered by the thought of the team, the good players, the Spazzes . . .

But there seems to be a sudden swingaround on the matter of Spazhood. The anger from people like Prince and Cody. Standing there in my bedroom, I'm struck by how unfair it is—I mean, here they are, getting a few gift goals from a completely unexpected source, and they're *angry* about something? I don't get it. Chill, boys. Just take those goals when they happen to come and count yourselves lucky. As I do. You can't *make* things like that happen.

So now, let's see . . . I look ahead to the final games, review scores, calculate our chances. We ought to win a few of these, maybe most of them. We ought to get killed a couple of times, too, but you never could tell—Zip could stop any team on any day, and some of our players could catch fire.

As I stand there yawning in my underwear, I have to admit the guilty secret that I could almost make a case, or at least a dream, for, well, for myself as a candidate to become one of those catch-fire players. My near-accidental gamewinner against York snapped something in my luck, there was no denying it. I started shooting all of those pucks I used to toy with, and also started seeking and finding more of them to shoot. More and more, I was getting my name hollered, my head swatted, my board-whack tribute from my fellow Spazzes.

I was having a lot of fun.

Does it sound as if my horizons had been

broadened, as recommended by the director of that music camp, or what?

I have to laugh. The fact is, like nothing I have ever run across, ice hockey just takes over once you let it into your life. No other sport played by anyone I know comes close. No other hobby.

But being a Spaz, I have kind of let hockey wash over me. I haven't, like, started devoting every waking thought to strategic variations on the breakout play or anything. And while it is true that I have let the level of my music slide, I was lucky in having had my mother feel she had just received the news that I was never going to be first-rate, so she has not been surprised at a little laxity. I guess she figured I ought to push as hard as possible as long as I had the chance to crack the top echelon (when I was about six, I was good enough to make such hopes reasonable). When it was clear my talent wasn't quite up to the highest challenges, well, I might as well relax a little. I am very grateful for this attitude, and though it is absolutely true, the fact is I also take advantage of it by "relaxing" music's hold on me a good deal more than is quite necessary. I get by. That's cool. If I find an oboe in my hands, it's like finding the puck on my forehand in the slot. I don't really think or ask questions anymore, or wonder how I got here and how I could get back again if I wanted to try. I just cash in.

This winter, a chamber music group I was invited to play in was putting together a long and difficult concert program to raise money for a children's hospital. There were seven other musicians, most of them more talented than me. Because everyone had a rigorous personal practice schedule, it was not easy to find times when we could rehearse together as an ensemble. There ended up being only seven sessions.

Three of them conflicted with hockey practices. Not *games*—just practices.

I skipped all three, and skated.

Thinking about it from the distance of a couple of months, I realize that maybe I could have at least split things up, two musics and one hockey, or even one music and two hockeys. But no. There was never a hesitation, even though I was still a completely *awful* hockey player. If there was a choice between hockey and *anything* else, hockey got the nod, every time. That's just how it felt right.

As it worked out, I played well in that concert, with a relaxed kind of flair I had never shown before. In fact, as I have slacked off a little, my music has gotten better in some ways. True, I miss more notes now, slip in my embouchure more, and I get tired more quickly. But there's a kind of easiness to the way I just up and play a piece now, blowing through the missed notes, feeling my way all the way through in one blow instead of breaking the technical challenges down into components. Much less work, much more surprising fun. I don't think my mother is displeased, and I am glad.

As for my father—well, the time I used to devote to church activities has definitely been iced. A minister's son is under pretty close watch in a church community, but my father has always made it clear to me that as far as he is concerned, I am under no pressure to be or do anything but what I am and believe in. I have missed some Sunday services during hockey travel weekends. I have had to give up something I enjoyed: being an assistant Sunday school teacher for kindergartners, because I could not commit every Sunday to church.

Recently I have not had any best-pal kind of

friendships in the church community, any more than I have in my music world. There is a group of guys my age that I used to spend more time with—we got together regularly to kind of study Scripture—but music had already taken me away from their intense focus on religious stuff. They are smart guys, and I gather that by now they have gotten pretty serious. If my father wanted to look at my withdrawal a certain way, sure, he could say that time spent skating after pucks has been time squandered. I think that's how a couple of the guys in the study group see it. But not my father. No way.

My grandfather, who was a Methodist minister too, once made a wise answer to a woman who was putting herself through agony about her sinfulness because she had realized suddenly, in the middle of an Alfred Hitchcock movie, that she had gone a long time without thinking about the Savior. My grandfather said, "God didn't give us a world with Alfred Hitchcock movies in it so we could ignore this man's genius for creating suspense, for captivating the mind completely in many shivery moments that, ultimately, thrill and delight us. Being alive," my grandfather said, "is supposed to be quite different from being deprived."

We have a game in exactly three hours. I can't believe I have come to a point where I can be so bold as to say this, but: I bet I score. I feel it in my hands. I *want* it. I want it *good*.

have been amazed during this season to notice how much adhesive tape is used per player per game. In a way, it makes sense to me to use sticky tape to attach things to each other, or to one's body; there is something direct and primitive about adhesive tape. It is not a device. It is sticky stuff made for sticking.

Ernie decided this year that he would take every piece of tape he used in the course of the season, and save it in the form of a solid sphere. The team made a $1-apiece pool on guessing how big the ball will be at the end of the year, but I am fascinated by the slow accretion, piece by unfolded piece, of a solid mass that looks so orderly and unified, when in fact Ernie, like all the players, wraps tape around his shin pads or socks with abandon, letting the tightly rolled tape loose in what seems like a chaos of wild fastening.

The sphere, right now, is about a third-again

bigger than a duckpin bowling ball. The other day, when no one was looking, I picked it up and gave it a heft. It surprised me with its weight, its density; it weighed *more* than the bowling ball would. A season's worth of work. . . .

n the first period, playing on a line with Shinny, who is increasingly one of our better passers, and Dooby, who has a fabulous shot from the point, I crash through a bunch of people toward the net just in time to see the goalie throw his leg pads in front of the puck whizzing at the net, a foot off the ice. The puck has not even dropped to the ice in its rebound before a sly stick blade darts between the legs of a defenseman from behind, and scoots it directly over to me. The defenseman, who is facing me, is still looking down where the rebound was *supposed* to land, as I sweep it into the net with a grandiose follow-through. Then I throw up my arms and collect all the swats and hollers and the proud cry—from only a single voice this time, which I don't stop to think about—"*Spaz! Spaz! Spaz!*"

"Man, that feels so *good!*" I holler to Shinny as we skate back toward center ice.

"Glad you enjoyed it," he says dryly.

"Hey, great pass, man—really, I mean, thanks."

"Don't thank me," he says, giving me a funny little half-smile. He gestures upward. "I didn't do it for you. I did it for the scoreboard, you know?"

"Sure," I say, with a grin. "But somebody's got to get it up there into the lightbulbs from the ice outside the cage."

"Well, I'm glad we have you around then." He smiles. "And I'm glad Dooby and I keep remembering to backcheck your man as he picks up speed to rush the zone. Hope we don't get excited and forget about him or anything. Or get boxed in fighting for the puck in the corners." He grins again, then bends to the face-off.

All right, so I hate the corners. There just seem to be people who are *good* at doing that, at throwing themselves toward the boards and spreading their skates and keeping one or even two frantic grabbing opponents on their hips while they try to create room down near the ice to manipulate their sticks and get a dominant hold on the puck—man, it's *exhausting* to me, I just plain stink at it, and the fact is, Shinny is correct, I stink at man coverage too. How am I supposed to keep track of one guy who is *trying* to hide from me, while I also attempt, to the last second of opportunity, to take advantage of my offense? Too much.

But it's a fabulous game for us. This is a New Jersey team that killed us twice, but on top of my goal Boot and Woodsie pile two more, and then the more the Jersey boys get concerned with handling the puck just right so they don't waste a chance to score, the more we hammer them in the open ice. At one point in the second period, their coach has to use his timeout just to settle his guys down because each of their *four* previous possessions ended with a winger sprung and whirled completely off the ice by a hipcheck at the blue line.

"Guess they'll finally start dumping it," says Coach Cooper with just the tiniest touch of indecent amusement. Then he reminds us of a few key moves against the dump-and-chase offense they are doomed to employ, and off we go. The timeout changes nothing; we keep eating them alive. In the last shift of the period Prince and Cody one-touch it from the red line in, looking like voodoo twins, against a single gutty but outclassed defenseman who keeps sweep-checking at *just* the wrong moment, until he falls, crossing over backwards in the slot, and barrels into his own goalie. Cody skeets to a stop with the puck, takes a good long look at the tangle, shakes his head disdainfully, then roofs it casually right before the buzzer.

Late in the third, I find myself with the puck, skating in hard with Shinny off to my right. At just the right moment, when the defenseman checking him cheats a look over my way to make sure his teammate has *me* covered, Shins tucks and dashes to the outside and cuts back in behind the guy, wide open. He looks for the pass. The goalie has committed to me and is way out. But instead of sliding it across to Shinny, I do not hesitate—I fire a shot, directly into the logo on the goalie's chest and he smothers the puck for no rebound.

"Nice move," I pant to Shinny as he cruises over, bent at the waist, stick across his knees, to the face-off dot.

Without straightening he looks up. "So?"

I half-laugh. "So what?"

"So where was the puck that I earned with my nice move?"

"You missed too many practices in the middle of the season," I say with a chuckle. "Coach's favorite phrase was, 'Shark—shoot it, shoot it, shoot it!'"

"Ah, I see." Shinny nods. "So *that* was his favorite."

"No, really." I say, "I'm just—"

"Maybe next he'll graduate to 'Shark—look, think, and then, maybe, *maybe*, shoot!'"

"No doubt you'd have buried it from where I was," I kind of snap.

He shakes his head. "Nope. Because I never would have shot it in the first place. Not with a forward so open. And not even if I were alone, unless I could get a better angle. Couldn't you see he had yours completely cut?"

"I guess I could." I pout. "But I'm a shooter now, and—"

"A 'shooter.' I see," Shinny says. "Not a Spaz, but a 'shooter' now."

"Well, you know what—"

"Shots," Shinny says, looking me in the eye appraisingly, and I realize with a shudder that he has just changed my name. "Well, better luck next time, Shotser."

Soon the game is over and we have absolutely whomped them, 6–0, Zip's fifth shutout. At one point early in the year, his goals-against average was certainly above 10.00.

"Great game, Zipster," I tell him with a head rub as we skate off after the handshaking.

"Was it, Shotsy?" he says, looking at me curiously. I try to ignore the fact that he has already adopted my disgusting new nickname.

"Well—sure!" I laugh. "I mean—"

"Recall any especially tasty saves, do you? Got any memories of this or that tough one to the glove side, a flutterer that required one of those incredible off-balance skate jobs of mine? Hmm?"

"Well, not exactly," I say, "but—"

He slings his arm around my shoulders. "Don't sweat it, Shots. As a matter of fact, there were none. No hard saves, not one. They only had nine shots on goal and every one of them was easy. But it's okay. You goal-scorers, when you get one in the net you can't help thinking it was a *great* game for everybody."

"If you'd prefer, I could start screening you for some of those easy shots," I say.

"Oh, you will." He grins. "You always do, Shots old fellow. In fact, I'd bet you never have any idea where you are standing, in terms of my line of vision and the puck. No idea at all. But, hey, you can't think of everything, right? And if I let one in off your idiotic screen, you'll get it back for me down ice, right?"

"I'm afraid you must be thinking of somebody else," I say with a small laugh.

"No, Shotsy, it won't work," he says, giving my shoulders a good wag. "Won't work. Can't do it."

I can't help asking. "Do what?"

"Get all stumble-humble again once you've gotten greedy." He gives me a wink. "But I like greed in my forwards, Shots. It works, better than almost anything."

He lets me go but I persist, bothered. "So what is it that works better? If I'm getting 'greedy,' as you say, I'd just as soon skip ahead to the better thing."

He laughs hard, for real. "Oh, man," he says, slowing down. "Oh, boy. The better thing? You'll figure it out when you're ready," he says. He laughs again. "Man, you—you're just *barely* entitled to a little bit of greed. You ought to be overcome with joy with *that* for a while, at least."

"I am," I say.

"I know." He winks at me. "Just remember, it ain't *everybody's*."

"*What* isn't everybody's?"

He laughs hard again. "Well, I don't know, let's see. Could it be . . . the joy? No, probably not. Who doesn't take joy from a—hey, that's it! The *goal*! The goal you score—that can't be everybody's, can it? It's yours, right? And you enjoy it, okay, Shots? And never mind those screens, *or* the corners." He laughs again, and moves away.

I am really troubled—I know Zip has just told me a lot, and I ought to piece it all together, with some of the other stuff that's been happening. But for the moment, arriving at the locker room, entering to one or two shouts of "King of the Former Spazzes!" and "Hot stick! Puck hog!," I am too preoccupied, too happy—and maybe too dumb, and too greedy—to think any more about it.

Because my dad is so busy I have gotten used to spending very little time with him alone. And for the same reason, I don't expect him to be very hip to what my problems of the moment might be—especially, as is the case now, when I don't understand them myself.

But while I am doing my homework—and trying *not* to think about hockey, which is a reverse of the way it has been all year—there's a tap on my door and it opens and there's my dad.

He says hello and without being asked takes a seat on my bed. My dad has been coming to more of my hockey games and stuff, but I'm never sure how much he gets and how much he misses. Tonight he surprises me by saying, "I'm just curious—but does your heaviness have anything to do with it?"

I stare at him blankly, with no idea what he is talking about. "With what?"

In a kind of carefree way he has picked up my algebra homework and is flipping through it. "With your new tendency to, I believe I heard another father call it, 'crash the net.' To skate straight to where that puck will probably end up, so you can knock it in the way you are doing."

"My weight? Um, sure, I guess my size—"

"Your teammates must be impressed with your fearlessness," he says, looking at me with a smile. "It's certainly what impresses me the most—you just work your way right into the crush—I bet they never expected so much from a first-year player."

"Dad, I haven't exactly been ruling the games out there."

He looks at me a little curiously. "No? I would have said you have ruled quite a few shifts, wouldn't you?"

I laugh. "I don't rule anything."

He thinks for a moment. "Let me ask you something."

I had been pretending to get back to my homework, but with obvious patience I say, "Okay. What is it, Dad?"

"Are you proud?"

I blink. "Of what?"

"Of starting the season as a nobody, and then eventually working your way to become an important member of the team."

"I'm afraid you're speaking entirely as a deluded father who completely overrated his kid's contribution," I say. "I appreciate it. But I have not become an 'important' member of this team, certainly not in any way that would justify the kind of pride you're asking about. So, the answer is 'No.' I'm happy enough just to finish the season pretty much as I started."

He studies me. "Few things," he says softly, "are less appealing, or more dishonest, than false humility, Sebastian. Are you—"

I throw my pencil down. "Look, *you're* the one making the claims that I'm such a hot hockey player—why does it have to be false of me to know it's not like that? Okay, okay, I lucked into some goals—"

"Luck," he says.

"Yes," I say heavily, "luck. But—"

"And what distinguishes 'luck' from, say, intentional and carefully learned skill that raises one into a new echelon on the team, is essentially that one is not in any way responsible for 'luck'? Is that correct? Luck just kind of happens, whereas becoming moderately *good* means becoming increasingly *aware*?"

I look at my chemistry text. "Okay, that's a fair definition."

"And you've just been 'lucky.'"

He put down my algebra. "I'm just curious, Sebastian—but when does 'luck' show a frequency consistent enough that you—or others—start to depend on it?"

"You can never count on it," I say. "Others can't either. They'd *better* not."

He nodded. After a minute, he said, "Are you afraid of anything, Sebastian? Instead of being proud, perhaps?"

"I prefer to think," I smiled, "that I am simply and truly humble. As we are taught."

"As we are taught," he repeated. He nodded, and pushed himself up off my bed. Then I felt his hands on my shoulders. "Well," he said, "I am not afraid to be proud, of you. And I am not afraid to utterly reject humility."

Both of us laughed at that. He slipped his hands from my shoulders after a squeeze, and went to the door. But before going, he turned and said, "There's nothing wrong with being afraid of responsibilities; the mistake is in denying them."

"I'll remember that when I get some," I said. "Besides my homework, that is."

He smiled. "I'll leave you to it, then."

"Thanks for coming in, Dad."

"My pleasure, son."

"But, Dad?"

"Yes?"

I started to write out the answer to a chemistry question. "I'd be very careful with that pride if I were you."

"I am," he said.

thirteen

t gets worse. All week in practice my teammates seem to take a special pleasure in calling me Shots, and every time I get one off they cheer all phony, until Coach Cooper tells them to shut up. When I mess something up—which I seem to do without knowing what I missed, at least half the time—they say nothing at all.

Or almost nothing. Once when I am standing on the low edge of the circle, the puck sails right past me into the corner, but I hesitate to go after it. Cody zooms by and manages to smile inquiringly through the masks between us, and says, "Pardon, Shots— mind if I get my elbows sharpened? No, no—don't trouble yourself!" and crashes his way between the butts of two much larger players, to scramble and scratch and poke and claw. For a second as I watch, his busy obsession reminds me of times when I used to play my oboe that way, and, thinking of my new relaxed attitude toward music, I catch myself frowning at Cody and thinking, "Yuck—so much *work*."

The thought freezes my skate blades to the spot.

I am a hockey player. I am, right now, playing hockey. At this moment. And—Lord, how did it happen?—I just had the actual thought, "Yuck—so much *work*."

I remember when work was all I could do. I remember sitting in my stinking sweaty gear after a humiliating practice and thinking, *believing*, "Hey— good job. You worked as hard as you could out there today." I remember trying to learn, paying attention to positions and who was whose responsibility; it seemed impossible to get, but I worked anyway.

Scoring goals had seemed even more impossible. But I'm doing that. I guess I thought I had just kind of skipped that work stuff in between.

Now I am *not* working. The horror of it hits me: I am a hockey player, a Wing, a former Shark—and I am just smiling lightly and skating around, waiting for a chance to grab a goal that will still seem a big gift and surprise.

Because I didn't work for it.

I watch as a speedy winger for the other team

comes swooping around the net, timing his zip through the space between me and the clot of people against the boards just right so that if he gets lucky and the puck pops out, he will pick it up at full speed and probably get himself a breakaway.

Sure enough, the puck pops out as if he had commanded it. And just as he is plucking it niftily onto his stick blade, I push myself through one heavy stride, raise my stick sideways with my hands far apart, and cross-check him so hard from the side that his helmet flies off and hits the glass above Zip's head. Zip looks up, watches it fall, and, as the referee whistles me off the ice into the penalty box, says, "Good one. In fact, *excellent*. That little scooter really *needed* that."

As I head for the penalty box, I think: Perhaps there's hope. Perhaps I can recall how to work. *And* score.

We lose the game by two goals. I do not score. But for the last two periods, I do not really concentrate on trying to. Instead, I head into the corners several times, where I labor mightily but without any effect, as the puck just keeps skipping from my boot to someone else's stick shaft to someone else's blade, but I hit it with *my* blade and it goes to someone *else's* boot . . .

I also leave the offensive zone earlier than usual on at least four occasions, because the center I am supposed to cover tries to cheat toward the blue line for a sendaway pass. One time he gets it, but I am there too, and although I can't possibly keep up with him I do manage to bother his takeoff enough that both defensemen get back, and he gets no rush to reward his sneakiness.

As I come off the ice after these shifts without results, no one speaks to me. But once Boot—Boot!—gives my helmet a single tap.

In the locker room, which is quieter because we lost, Cody, fooling with his tape player, stutter-steps as he passes me and says, "Great cross-check, Shots."

"It was," says Prince, looking up at me as briefly as possible.

But I hear only the word *Shots.* And I know there is still a lot of work to be done.

fourteen

One day before one of our last practices, Cody suddenly says to me, "Is it hard to play that oboe deal?"

"Well, yes, actually it's considered one of the hardest, among the wind instruments at least, mostly because it has two very stiff but thin reeds—"

"How long did it take you to get good?"

I think. "I don't know. But—I know it sounds weird after I just finished saying how difficult it is— when I was about five or six it just all of a sudden seemed very easy and natural to me." I shrug.

"Like skating for you, Codes," says Woodsie, who is a determined but awkward skater openly envious of Cody's unconscious grace.

"Or singing for Prince," says Barry.

"That also takes a *lot* of work," says Prince without looking up from the skate he is tying.

"So does everything, even the stuff that you

suddenly find you are able to do," says Cody lightly. But no one follows his comment, and I imagine them all mentally adding: *Such as scoring a few goals, Shots my lad.*

Without thinking, I say, "I think Harrisonville will be scared of us Saturday."

A few guys look at me with interest. Harrisonville is an excellent team of big, very skilled players. At the moment, they have lost only to Montrose, twice, and are thus in the hunt for the league title.

Finally, Woodsie says, "Because they will think we have nothing to lose and will play crazy and be creative and so on?"

I nod. "And physical. They'll be afraid of getting hurt—they play Montrose on the last day of the season—and they'll think we'll be all reckless and carefree and smash into them whenever we can, whoopee!"

Prince looks up and considers. "You may be right," he says, giving me a look.

Dooby says, "That's one we're supposed to lose. Today was one we were supposed to win. Maybe we can switcheroo."

"That would be sweet," says Barry. "I'd hate to help Montrose, but, hey, we *already* beat them. For us, what's left of the season doesn't have anything to do with standings and stuff. We should just forget who is where, and kick everybody's tail. Just like"—he gestures toward me—"he says."

"You may call him Corners now," says Zip. "He seems to have lost his scoring touch, and with it, alas, his greed. Now all he does is make a mess wherever the puck goes."

"Corners is better than Shots," I hear myself saying, and cannot believe I have the guts to speak up. "But it's a long way from Shark." I look Zip right in the eyes.

He smiles. "So eat a few people," he says. "Easy."

"It wouldn't hurt to score a couple of goals while you're at it," says Dooby. In our last three games we have a total of four.

Zip buries his head in his hands. "I can't *believe* this hockey team has fallen so low that it is begging for goals from someone who started the season thinking the puck was made of wood."

"Well," I say, acting offended, "how are you sup-posed to tell if you've never been close to one? I mean, it's hard; it's, like, kind of *carved* into this shape—"

"And be careful when you beg him for goals, Zip," says Prince. "Remember—he almost scored one on you."

"Had it in my sights the whole way," Zip says.

"But that was before I started playing with the heavily curved stick," I say, and there is general laughter. Pure shooters curve their sticks to get extra spin on their forehand shots. The curve hurts their puckhandling and backhand shot or pass, however.

Zip laughs about the curved stick too, genuinely. "Ah, Corners," he says. "Maybe there is hope."

After just a second's pause, Barry says, "Yeah, well, at least let's do what he says to those pretty boys from Harrisonville."

"Tell me, Barry," says Dooby, frowning seriously. "Do you sometimes find yourself . . . well, *attracted* to these young men?"

"Reston has a gay guy playing for them," says Cody.

"No way!" say several players. Cody just waits them out. "It's that defenseman, Number 12. He just announced it one day, and said nobody on the team had to worry about anything because they were all hideous." Cody shrugs. "Who cares? I mean, what's the big deal once he puts his skates on?"

If it were anyone but Cody, a caustic series of answers would have followed. As it is, everyone knows very well he means it—he really *doesn't* think it's a big deal—and however Cody came up with that who-cares attitude, it ought not to be impossible for us; in any case, no one is going to argue at the moment, and several guys even imitate his shrug, probably unconsciously. Woodsie says, "He's a very good player."

"Tell me, Woodsie," says Dooby, frowning even more deeply. "Do you sometimes find yourself—"

"We'll do it," says Prince, who has been so quiet we all forgot him.

"Do what?" says Barry.

"Play Harrisonville crazy and whup them, and maybe there will even be a goal for this fat person across from me who now must suffer the miserable shame of having lost such a sweet name as Shark."

"What do you think, Boot?" Ernie asks.

The Boot, struggling a little with the zipper on

his bag, does not look up, but merely says, "As names and such things go, the Boot has always had a special feeling about the name 'the Boot.'"

Prince steps onto a bench. "And now," he says, "I will sing to us all."

He sings a song called "Mack the Knife." There's a shark in it. And a lot of blood.

fifteen

No one can go nuts quite like Cody. Or maybe I should say, no one can go so nuts he seriously alarms you *and* play incredible hockey at the same time like Cody. On the first shift against Harrisonville, as the puck skitters to him off the face-off, he inverts his stick the way teams working on body-position defense sometimes do in practice, gripping it with the blade under his arm and just the skinny little upper tip on the ice to handle the puck. Nevertheless, handle it he does, skating quickly through the entire Harrisonville team as they stand still and watch, before deking the goalie to the center and tucking the puck inside the near post.

"Okay, Hawks," hollers their coach, not sounding especially mad or anything. "It works just once, all right?"

But it is all we need. With the lead we really loosen up and act as if we didn't care about anything, least of all our bones and joints and large muscle groups. We hurl ourselves at them and knock them right off their slightly uptight game. I have a wonderful time cleaning house in the corners, just forgetting about the puck and trying only to make certain I am the last player left standing within fifteen feet. And—as if he had been saving it all year—even Prince delivers a flawlessly timed, devastatingly placed hipcheck against their top scorer, who had hypnotized himself with his own fancy stickhandling. The kid goes off the ice in the middle of the second and never comes back.

I get to handle the puck only once, but it is in a scoring position. I am late leaving the offensive zone because their defenseman has a hold on the shaft of my stick, so when Cody intercepts a pass in the high circle, I need only loop back and take his pass and there I am, alone facing the goalie.

Cruising in with the puck on my forehand, I smile into the goalie's eyes. "Consider yourself eaten," I say, showing some teeth, and draw back my stick. He flops into the butterfly. I rather sloppily draw a pass back through my legs to where I hope Cody is, and the next thing I see is the puck whistling past me into the string.

Prince skates up and peers into my mask, looking at my mouth. Finally, he nods.

"What?" I say.

"You do have pretty teeth, dear," he says. "When you show them, so pearly white."

sixteen

Our usual schedule for a week-end was to play two games on Saturday and one on Sunday. It was the same when we traveled—we all just got up early and drove to the morning game on Saturday and met there, or some people went up and spent Friday night in whatever town our morning game was in. In addition to these weekend games, we had an occasional game around seven on a weeknight, but the leagues know they have to be careful about cutting into time parents see as exclusively slotted for homework.

I mentioned before that my father had started coming to more of my games, especially Saturday games. Naturally, I never expected him to come on the Sabbath—frankly, I was grateful he let *me* play on what had always been *his* hardest workday but which, in our family's vocabulary of pretense, was soberly referred to as "the day of rest."

Even Saturdays, I knew, were packed for my father, what with the weddings and funerals and memorial services. There was always a fiftieth-anniversary party it would be *so* nice if the Reverend could drop in on, or an engagement luncheon which, if he could just stop by, just for *dessert*, or even a quick cup of coffee, well, the young people would feel *so* blessed. So many people in the community, and all of them had some need for him, it seemed, and usually on Saturday.

Also, when it came to the privileges of the pulpit, my father very thoughtfully wrote, and rewrote, and rewrote his own sermons, and it was not unusual to find him finally settling down to this work as the rest of us were getting ready for bed.

Riding home once I said, "You're coming to a lot of my games. How do you like this game?"

He thought for a second or two, then said, "I find it all very interesting."

Ah. "You mean, you look around at all these people and marvel at how much energy they put into this world you never knew existed?"

He wrinkled his forehead. "No, what I find most interesting is . . . well—" he laughed "—looking out over the surface of that ice and going from young man to young man until, all of a sudden, with a wonderful sensation that is partly thrill and partly something like shock, I find . . . I find one young man with his name across his shoulders and I realize it is the same name I bear, and then I have to recognize further that this young man, out there doing things I never taught him, things I could never even approach doing myself, is my very own son."

He looks over at me and I nod. He goes back to looking ahead, through the car's windshield, and says, "Now, I am going to tell you something that you must do your best not to misunderstand, not to interpret in such a way that it makes me sound as if I am—"

"I know," I say. "You couldn't get into the oboe."

His head snaps toward me and his face is like a bad actor's freeze of "Alarm." "You *knew?*" he whispers hoarsely.

"Sure, and don't worry about it, because it never took anything away from my own feelings, or Mother's, nor did it affect my ability to perform. With that oboe in my hands, I always knew I was on my own, and as much as I appreciated the support you two gave me—and I mean the support you *both* gave, equally; giving support doesn't depend on 'liking' for yourself what you are supporting for someone else, right?—I felt completely happy being alone up there on stage."

He has started nodding rapidly, his face struggling between relief at his confession and excitement that I am leading to a point I guess he wants to make about hockey. Finally he can't stand it and cuts me off.

"Yes!" he says. "You *are* alone, and yet *not* alone, because—this sounds so strange!—because I am privileged to be there *beside* you. Not *inside*, but just alongside, closer up than anyone else can ever get, except, of course, your mother—but it is as a *witness* to your individual joy that I find myself fulfilled to be a father. To be *your* father."

This is pretty strong stuff, and we ride for a long time on it like a full tank of gas. Then, just as we are approaching our neighborhood, he says a last thing.

"Do you want to know something?"

"Sure."

He licks his lips discreetly, eager to express a

fine point finely. "It is this. For all of my—feeling so inextricably close to this utterly other person who is you, there *is* a time when I strangely lapse a bit, when I kind of fall back a little, when I find myself less attached." He is almost frowning now.

"I'm sure that's natural," I say. And then I ask: "When is it that this happens?"

"Well," he says, and changes his frown into a quick laugh of incredulity, "oddly enough, it is when you are at the height of your individual glory—that is, when you put in a goal. Not because of all the celebration—that I find most congenial. But . . . there's just something that strikes me as a tiny bit off, inside you. And I feel for a second that I don't know you then. That you vanish." He is frowning again, but as we pull onto our street he smiles. "But you always come back."

I am a little shaken, but I try to joke through it. "You mean I fall down, or run into somebody, or skate over the blade of my stick and take a huge comic spill, or something like that? Something more typical of my unique combination of hockey skills?"

He is shaking his head the whole time. When I

finish, he says, quietly and firmly, "No, son. No. Not at all. As I have tried to tell you . . . it seems as natural now for you to score a goal as it used to for you to display some beginner's awkwardness." He thinks, and finally gives up, shaking his head. "What I feel is something else. It's"—he shrugs— "it's something I hear from inside you. Maybe some doubt, maybe some reticence, maybe some self-indulgence—some completely understandable and minor discomfort. That's all. Probably I'm wrong. Probably there is no such moment of mysterious misgiving. Probably your joy is complete."

He lets it hang there as a nonquestion. So do I. We arrive at home, and get out, and go about our separate evenings, all without speaking of this intuition of his. In fact, we will almost certainly never speak of it. But we both know he is right. And at least one of us is pretty worried about it.

seventeen

So, for the final game of the season, my name is restored. It happens almost unnoticeably; Prince mutters a French Canadian cussword as his tape runs out in the middle of a sock, and he says, "Shark—give me some tape."

I toss him a half-roll, and say nothing. Feel rather a lot, though.

For this game I play once again with Shinny. And in the first period, as if it were the movies and I was being given a chance to redeem myself, I am carrying the puck down the left wing two-on-two, and Shinny works the same nifty little sneak move to get open when his defender peels at me, and just like before, he looks to me for the pass. But this time the *goalie* steals a quick look at *Shins*, so I shoot again, but now I do not hit the goalie in the logo on his sweater. I do not hit him anywhere. He never sees the puck as it pops through the five-hole at just the moment his eye is on Shins.

"I suppose that was a fair shot," Shinny says, giving my helmet a rub. "But I worked pretty hard for nothing."

"You know better," I say.

"What?" he says.

I try to sound mock-pompous. "In hockey, one's work is *never* for 'nothing.'"

"Tell it to my dad," Shinny says. "He said he'd get my guitar neck adjusted if I scored a goal."

"It just so happens," I say, "that the neck is perfectly straight exactly as it is. So you see—"

We win the face-off, Woodsie rushes it over the blue and pulls up abruptly and fires a terrific shot the surprised goalie stops with the bouncy center part of his fat leg pad. The rebound shoots right up the slot to Shinny, who simply flips it in. For a quick second, so only I can see, he pretends to play his stick like a guitar.

"Maybe it needs a *little* torque around the octave marks," I say.

It is not until the break between the second and third periods that Zip makes his only appearance of the season in the bench huddle, instead of skating straight down the ice to the opposite goal, sticking his tongue out at the other goalie the whole way.

"Listen up," he says. We all look at him, including Coach Cooper. Zip gives us each a sincere study. "This is—well, it's kind of a special game," he says.

"Why is that, oh Zip?" Cody asks.

"Because," Zip says. He looks around at us, his expression growing slightly more passionate as he speaks. "Do you *realize?* That if we *win* this *game,* then, if you take all of the games we have lost by more than five goals and subtract them from the number of Fridays that have passed us by this year, *and* divide the resulting subtrahend—" He cocks an eyebrow at the coach. "You like that? Subtrahend? Do goalies rule, or what?"

"Goalie, take your net," calls the ref from center ice.

"Coming," Zip says. "Anyway, then—and again, this is only if we *win* this game, *win only,* a clear out-and-out *victory,* more *goals* than them, you know?—then the number we come up with, the number we get to treasure through those long summer months, the number we frankly had no right to hope for as late as five weeks into the season—"

"Goalie!"

"—is eight," Zip finishes. He gives us a wink and says, "Think about it. Think about a little something to be proud of when the sun is beating—"

"Goalie, I'm going to call you for delay!"

"Eight," Zip repeats. "Don't forget." Then he puts his head down, skates full speed for the cage, and skeets to a perfect stop with his mask less than an inch from the crossbar. He waves his stick at the ref.

"Ready, Your Honor," he says.

My second goal happens so fast I barely register it. One second their defenseman is skating across the slot with the puck and I am forechecking; the next second I snap his stick up and flick the puck with my backhand, almost in one motion, and it hits the inside of the far post and stays in.

When I pass him on the bench at the end of the shift, Prince says, "Nothing in the bestial crudity of the animal kingdom is quite so disgusting as a feeding frenzy."

"You're the one who had to go and sing about blood," I say. "Those songs—they get a fella to thinkin'."

The other team scores a goal that would make it 3–1 after Boot nets a pretty wrister for us, but the ref waves their score off.

"*Why?*" screams the center who scored, obviously with his skate.

"*So I can preserve my shutout, that's obviously why, you moron,*" Zip screams back at exactly the same volume. The center wheels away, without another protest.

He does preserve it. In the last six minutes we play careful defensive hockey for the first time in the game. Nobody—except, of course, Boot—is thinking about scoring. We just keep them frustrated at our blue line, keep banging the puck off the boards through the neutral zone and making them chase it to their own end, keep Zip's sight lanes clear when they do set up on offense, keep the men in the slot tied up.

Nevertheless—I'm on again for the game's final shift, the final shift of the season, in fact—nevertheless, with about fifteen seconds left a careless pass hits my left skate by accident and caroms perfectly so that I follow it and pick it up on my backhand and there I am, no one closer behind me than twenty feet, the goalie disheartened and already starting to flop, hardly raising his blocker, and I have the puck, and two goals, two of 'em in the last game of my first season in this incredible sport, and for the last thirty feet everyone on the bench has been screaming *"Hats! Get the hats!"* and I think of what a wonderful sound "hat trick" has to it, implying just that degree of cunning as it does, and as the goalie sinks to the right I move easily to the left, make certain the puck is flat against my stick, and, with an easy-feeling, natural-born, almost carefree but technically perfect motion, I lose the puck as if I owned it, and it snaps off my stick just right, and squarely, with a perfect metallic sound, hits the post. I hit the post, with a two-foot wrist shot—a shot that would have gotten me a hat trick. I can only watch in horror as the puck rolls on its edge past me to the lonesome corner, and the buzzer sounds.

My teammates spring from the bench like a single animal and rush toward me, hooting and shrieking, hollering *"Ding!"* and *"Hold the chapeaux!"* which of course must be Prince, and I try to look dignified and start a quickly improvised speech about deciding at the very moment temptation was put before me to remain humble in a manner appropriate to my seniority on the team, but they overwhelm me and send me flying backwards. Out of the corner of my mask I even see Zip, all the way down the ice from his cage where we usually rush to *him*, leaping onto the top of the mound of padded bodies.

And now they are all saying one thing. In fact, they are chanting it: *"Shark!"* they bark. *"Shark! Shark! Shark!"*

And I remember, from my hodgepodge of biology facts, or myths, that a shark must never stop swimming; all the time, it's swim swim swim. It strikes me that after a while, at least sometimes, swimming is just another kind of work, right?

sit in the locker room, staring at the ice skate that still stays on my left foot, and I feel that I cannot take it off. This is a strange and compelling feeling, but it's not the only thing making up my disposition at the moment—I am also seized by a profound gloom, a cranky sense of some vague injustice being worked against me, a kind of impersonal grief, and a nagging sense that I have lost something.

"Feelin' pretty good, hmm, Sharky?"

I look over my shoulder. It is Prince. He too is only partly undressed. A few minutes ago, after we left the ice and the jolliness of our victory and my messed-up hat trick, Prince, all of a sudden, stood up in the silence, as if to sing as usual; but after a moment he shook his head and said, "No tune today" and sat back down. So I know something bothers him too.

"What *is* it?" I ask him. We look around the

room. No one is smiling. Everyone is dawdling. Zip is paying such close attention to each buckle on his pads that one would think he had never handled them before. Even Cody just sits, slouched backward against the wall, no equipment removed other than his mouthguard.

"Let me ask you something, Shark." It is Dooby, who seems to be maintaining his keen awareness, but who also seems subdued.

"Sure."

"If we were a football team, or a baseball team, or a basketball or volleyball or wrestling team, and we had just finished a tough season with a victory that shows we have come a long way, beating a much better opponent, well, would we be feeling, say, a little festive?"

I look at Prince. "Sure, I guess. I mean, I haven't ever played a season of a sport before—"

"We would be festive all right," says Java, who played football for several years. "It would be a party in here. Everybody'd be all proud and satisfied and have this great feeling of well-earned, like, accomplishment, and all this energy would be letting go and bouncing all over the place."

"He's right," says Cody, without unslouching. Cody plays lacrosse in the spring. "The end of a season is always a big celebration."

I look around. "So what's wrong with us?"

Barry finally strips off the sock he has been contemplating. "This was a *hockey* season," he says. As if that explains it as well as it could be explained, nearly everyone nods.

"But . . . I mean, so? A hockey season is over. Big deal. I feel like I just died," I say.

"*Now* you got it," says Dooby.

"But I *don't*," I say. Then I think of something. "What about last year for you guys? You won everything that could be won. You were the best, had the most to be happy about and proud of. Was it different then, when *that* one was finished?"

Several heads shake, and Dooby says, "It was exactly the same."

Prince taps me on the shoulder. "I think it's simple. When a hockey season ends, you cannot feel anything but a complete sense of loss."

Heads nod.

"Loss?" I say, and recognize that he nailed it

perfectly—that's *just* what I am feeling. "But what have we lost?"

Everyone looks at me for an instant as if I were nuts. Then I guess they remember I am new to this, and soften back into their gloom, leaving it to Prince to explain the obvious.

"What have we lost?" he repeats. I nod. He smiles sadly. "We have lost hockey."

I start to say something, but then I stop, and think. It is true that in most sports, a season is like a story, and you go through it with a sense of it building to something that will close it off and make you happy or at least satisfied in some way. But—

"See," says Cody, as if he were reading my mind, "in all those other sports, the point is always to, like, get *through* a game, and get out with another win, and keep winning and stuff. There is always a point, and the point is to *get* somewhere."

"In what way is hockey so different?"

"It's not," says Barry, peeling his second sock. "It's just that the only place we want to get is—"

"—the ice," Dooby says.

Barry nods. "We just want to start playing. *That's* the point."

Woodsie is standing with his arms crossed, shoulders against the wall. His helmet is still half on, which makes him look like some mysterious sage. He says, "Playing. Just playing, that's the point. In a way, it's the 'ending,' the way other teams work toward an ending. The beginning—starting to skate—is the only 'goal' we have."

Dooby is nodding, as is Prince. Prince asks me, "Has this happened to you? When you go through the gate and get both skates on the ice and start to move—long before warmups, *long* before the opening face-off, or the third period, or the buzzer at the end—at that first moment, do you ever think, 'Whatever happens, this is *it*.'"

I can only nod.

"We all want to win," Dooby says. "It's not like we let go and groove on 'just being here.' But if you gave any hockey player who's a real hockey player the choice between a forfeit victory—no game—against a team that was going to kick your tail and beat you by ten goals, if you said 'You can have that victory and you don't even have to tie your skates' and the other choice was to go ahead and play the game and get crushed, well, a hockey player would not hesitate. He'd tie his skates and say 'Drop the puck and let's get going.'"

I ask, "Do you guys go through this very same thing every year, after the last game?"

The more experienced players laugh. Everyone nods. Cody says, "My dad, every year when the season ends, he turns into a *total* redass for like two weeks and then one day he comes to dinner smiling and announces that we are going to move. He's going to get a new job, and the whole family is going to move to Canada. Because there's like six days between the end of spring hockey and the start of fall hockey up there."

"Even Coach feels it?"

Cody nods.

"But—well, you're still here."

"Yeah," Cody says. "Well, you just keep breathing and eating and going to sleep and eventually the off-season is over. Besides, the fast food is weird in Canada—no offense, Prince; besides, you don't like fast food anyway—and they don't have Dr Pepper up there."

"Which evidence of cultural inferiority has always kept in check your father's drive to emigrate,

no doubt," says Prince. "That, and the fact that tem-
peratures drop to seventy below in some places. It's
hard even to want to go outside and pass the ol'
puck around at seventy below."

"Speaking of food," says Cody, starting to take
his stuff off, "and speaking of things getting bleak
for the immediate future, did anybody see that they
closed the Donut Dinette two weeks ago and in the
same place this morning they opened—"

"*Don't say it!*" screams Zip, putting his hands
over his ears. "*Don't say that word!*"

"What word?" asks Cody, looking at him.

"Starbucks, of course," Zip says calmly. "Never
speak that word to me."

"My dad has been getting fresh donuts from the
Dinette at least a few times a week since he was our
age," says Cody. "When we passed there this morning it wasted him bad."

Dooby cups one hand beside his mouth and
rises on his tiptoes and leans to holler over to where
we are sitting. "Oh Prince! I was wondering if perhaps, once our obligatory period of transitional
gloominess is over this morning, you might care
to join me for, ooh, let's see, I think, yes, a grande

macchiato, with a light dusting of cinnamon? Sound luscious? Starbucks also has those *fabulous* tiny danishes that look like they were glazed with floor wax and go for about three seventy-five. If we save up, we should be able to split one of those, too, by August."

"No thanks, Doobs," says Prince. "But I do think we ought to do the pool business on Ernie's tape ball, to which I see he has just applied his final piece."

"Yup," says Ernie, looking at the large sphere on the floor between his feet. "She's pretty, isn't she?"

Woodsie finds the pool entries while Dooby and Ernie get the ball's measurements. No one is at all excited about the whole show, and when Java wins and Woodsie hands him a large wad of one-dollar bills, he looks at the cash as if it were a handful of earthworms and says, "I don't want to spend this."

"You could afford two of those danishes at Starbucks," someone says and a couple of people laugh.

Java says, "Is there some way I can, like, spend it on the team?"

No one can think of any way. Zip kills any speculation about getting in a little extra hockey by telling us flatly that the amount Java holds would not pay for even a half-hour of ice time.

Java puts the money down on the floor between his bag and Billy's.

"You know what this feels like?" Ernie, bereft of his sphere, says.

"What?" Woodsie answers.

"Well, it's one of those times when you have to just shrug and say 'Hockey is different.' It reminds me of the time I was at a cousin's house and a pro football game was on the television, and it ended, and—I couldn't believe it, I went nuts saying 'This is crazy! What are they *doing*?'—and right there, on the field, the players from both teams just *ran* over to each other, and started hugging and smiling and talking like the best of friends. I mean, these guys had been out on that same field a few minutes before, trying to *kill* each other, and now suddenly they're all buddies." Ernie shakes his head.

Barry makes a sign of deep disgust. Zip says, "Try to imagine the guys from another hockey team coming over to us after the phony handshake line, and trying to hug us."

"They would die," says the Boot quietly. "On the spot."

Ernie goes on. "I don't mean to say I think football is for good sports and hockey is for bad sports. That's not how it is at all. There are some things you do or don't do in a game, that represent 'good sportsmanship.' I guess the football hug-stuff is sending people the message that, like, your opponent need not be your enemy, or something."

A lot of players chuckle and shake their heads at such craziness. Because in hockey, it is clear: Your opponent is most definitely your enemy. You despise him, you want to crush him, humiliate him, hit him fair and clean—no one wants injuries—but hard, and, after the game is over, throw him away like the wrapper of a candy bar. You don't want to shake his hand. You would *never* feel like smiling at him. And hugging?

The door opens and Coach Cooper strolls in. "You guys feel like crap because you can't play hockey for a while, I feel like crap because I can't coach hockey for a while, we're all miserable, that's the way it is, and I'm certainly not going to make things one bit better by giving some encouraging speech. It sucks that the season is over, and that is that."

"Well, gee, Coach," says Zip, "thanks for dropping by, really."

The coach waves a piece of paper at us. "For those of you who are new to this game, I hope you won't be disappointed to learn that hockey teams don't have end-of-season barbecues or nice award dinners where every player gets something and we celebrate losing twenty-nine games. Instead—"

"That's what we lost this year?" Zip asks, looking excited. "We only lost twenty-nine?"

"That's right," the coach says, and as Zip thrusts both fists out in what seems to be a gesture of genuine joy, he goes on. "It might be worth noting for a moment that your victory today kept you from losing thirty games on the season, which, by the way, would have set a new record of futility, for the entire Wolfbay club, in its entire history. So, yes, Zip, that is something to feel good about."

Woodsie, from the far corner, calls out, "And the

record, even though we failed to lose thirty, is what, Coach?"

The coach looks over at him in mild disgust. "You'll just never learn to leave it alone, will you, Woodsie?" He sighs. "The record is twenty-nine losses."

"So you mean we won that game today and *still* held on to our record?" Zip asks eagerly. "Those chumps we beat didn't cheat us out of our all-time record? We still got it? We got enough?"

"Yes, Zip, I'd say twenty-nine defeats is quite enough."

"*Yesss!*" says Zip, with another two-fisted thrust. "*Go, Wings!*"

"*Go, Wings!*" everyone shouts.

The coach just shakes his head. "Okay, whatever you say. In case it contributes further to your happiness, Zip, you might like to know that we *nuked* the record, that we flat *own* getting whomped as a statistical matter. Until now, the mark was a mere nineteen losses, sustained by the 1977 Bantam B team."

"My older stepbrother was on that team," says Shinny. He grins maliciously. "Wait till I tell him how bad we erased 'em."

"As I was saying," the coach continues, "it is not our custom to make any feeble attempt at enjoying our temporary deprivation of hockey by holding a nerdy barbecue or an even nerdier awards presentation. This, right here, is our awards presentation. An award really means nothing to anyone but your teammates anyway, so—"

"You mean we don't get, like, trophies and stuff?" says Billy, looking mournful and close to tears.

"Trophies are for bowling teams, Billy," Dooby says, not unkindly.

"Your dad will buy you a trophy," says someone else. Billy's father, who claims—often, and in a loud voice—to have spent a couple of years knocking around a few pro football teams as a utility player, is generally disliked, and well known for buying Billy the very latest, most expensive equipment and delivering long lectures on why whatever the rest of us are wearing is now obsolete and downright foolhardy. I have always felt sorry for Billy.

"No trophies," says the coach. "Okay, first off, the only award we give that isn't a matter of pure stats: Most Improved Player. Let's see . . . Boot, why don't you tell us who probably won this one?"

Boot says, "Woodsie, unless he got cheated."

"The awards committee, the voting member-ship of which consists of myself and myself alone, is *not* in the habit of cheating people, so, yes, you are correct, Woodsie is indeed the winner of the award, signified physically by absolutely nothing, no trinket, but which carries the far greater signifi-cance of the team's respect and reliance on your greatly increased responsibilities as the year pro-gressed. Congratulations."

"Thanks," says Woodsie. "Thanks to everybody for teaching me so much."

"You're certainly welcome," says Zip. "And, hey, Woodsie—any*thing*, any*time*, know what I mean, bro? Just ask."

"Next," says Coach, looking at his paper, "the award for the team's top goal scorer. Gotta finish those chances, guys. This year's winner, with forty-seven big ones, is Boot. Congrats, and may you get twice as many next year."

"Thanks for the setups, guys," says Boot.

"Which mention of setups brings us to what the awards committee refers to as the Prince award. This honor goes to the player who leads the team in assists for the season, the team's supreme master of the pass, who sometimes ignores perfectly beautiful shots in order to do his thing, but what the heck, in many more cases the winner of the Prince award uses his uncanny sense of the ice and the players on it, as well as his sometimes regrettable unselfishness, to create scoring chances where no one else could have foreseen one. Surprisingly enough, this year the Prince award goes to . . . Prince."

There is applause. Prince stands for no more than a quarter second.

"Lastly," says the coach, "we come to our only award the winning of which is determined entirely by genetic good fortune. This is the overall scoring award, goals plus assists, and the winner this year, with his inimitable speed and style and anticipation, is our captain, your son and mine, Cody."

Big applause and hoots. Cody clasps his hands and waves them above his head like a boxer.

"It's true," he says. "I rule. I am nothing less than the *caliph*."

"The what?" says Billy.

"Cody is using a word," says the coach, "which is the title borne by the ruler of, I believe, Egypt in ancient times, a word which—had he been able to come up with it during his final history exam— would have squeaked him to a D and thus saved him the terribly unpleasant time that he must soon begin spending, without air conditioning, in summer school. I imagine it's a word he will never forget."

"So what *did* you answer, Codes?" says Zip. "What did you say the ruler of Egypt was called?"

"Easy," says Cody. "'The Genie.'"

Big laughter. The coach begins to circulate among the players, shaking each one's hand discreetly and saying a few specific good things. I don't remember a word of what he says to me other than "See you in the fall for Peewees." I had never actually considered any future in hockey, but now that I do, it seems absurd that I might play only one season and be satisfied.

One by one, players drift out. I notice that no one says good-bye with any more ceremony than the usual, when you know you'll see the guy the next night at practice or two days later at a game. Finally, after Shinny leaves with a wave of the paper-thin cast on his wrist, only Prince and I—and the tape ball—remain.

"Java forgot his prize," Prince says, pointing to it in the middle of the floor. "What could *we* do with it, Sharkie?"

"Well," I say, "we could make it *symbolize* something, if we wished to. It's white but dirty, it's round but irregularly so, it smells bad—the possibilities are endless."

"I think we'll just leave it where it is," he says.

"In that case," I say, standing up and slinging my bag, "because for some strange reason I do not fancy being alone with it in the room, I will say good-bye." I take the three steps to the door and open it. "See you, Prince."

"See you, Shark," he replies. Then, as I step into the hallway and spot my father at the far end, apparently having a nice conversation with Dooby's dad, I hear Prince's voice, just making it out through the rapidly closing aperture of the door. "See you for Peewees, Shark. Be there."